Overboard

Overboard

ERIN THOMAS

NATIONAL LIBRARY OF CANADA CATALOGUING IN PUBLICATION DATA

Thomas, E. L. (Erin L.)
 Overboard / E.L. Thomas.

ISBN 978-1-926847-25-2

 I. Title.

PS8639.H572O94 2012   jC813'.6   C2011-908542-9

General editor: Paul Kropp
Text Design: Laura Brady
Illustrations by: Charlie Hnatiuk
Cover design: Robert Corrigan

1 2 3 4 5 6 7   17 16 15 14 13 12

Printed and bound in Canada

High Interest Publishing acknowledges the financial support of the Government of Canada through the Canada Book Fund for our publishing activities.

An accident at sea leaves Tanner in a lifeboat
with his kid sister and a guy he really despises.
The survival of the group depends on their
working together. But as the hot sun beats
down and the water runs out, their chances
don't look good.

The author would like to thank: Skipper Allan Riggs and his beautiful sailboat, *Bullet*; Erin Bennett and the other helpful people at the Whitby Yacht Club; Captain Wayne Andrew of Andrew's Charter Fishing in Port Credit; and Vivian Gauer for her first-hand knowledge of sailing life.

Contents

Chapter 1

The Sparta

We'd only seen the boat on a website. The *Sparta* – that was the name of the boat. She had looked pretty good on-screen. With her tall mast and white sails, she looked like a boat that could handle anything. Maybe even the four of us.

But the real *Sparta* didn't measure up.

The real *Sparta* was short and dumpy. Compared to the other boats lined up along the dock, the *Sparta* looked . . . yellow. Like bad teeth. This boat was going to take us to the Bahamas?

"That's it?" asked my ten-year-old sister Amy. She looked up at me over her wire-framed glasses.

"Yeah!" I said, forcing a grin. "Isn't it great?"

Amy tugged at her backpack. She didn't need to answer. Amy had made it pretty clear that she wasn't thrilled about being the only girl on board. There wasn't going to be much room on the tiny ship. And it was at least a three-day trip.

Dad was way behind us, about halfway down the dock. He kept looking over his shoulder. Even farther back, at the top of the dock, was Cory, the son of Dad's girlfriend. Cory's nearly a year older than me. And about as lively as a dead worm.

I could tell that Dad didn't want to leave Cory too far behind. But he didn't want us to get too far ahead either. Dad was caught in the middle.

Yup, we were one big, happy family. Me, Dad, Amy . . . and Cory.

I looked at the *Sparta*. Then I looked back at Amy. "We should wait," I said.

"For Dad? Or for the Slug?" she asked, walking on. Slug was her nickname for Cory. She liked him about as much as I did.

I laughed, then stopped myself because I knew something Amy didn't. "We shouldn't call him that any more," I said, catching up with her. After all, we were going to be stuck with this guy for three days.

And maybe a long time after that.

"Why not?"

But just then, we reached the boat. There was no time to answer. Which was good, because I didn't want to tell her about the engagement ring. I'd found the ring in Dad's coat pocket.

Dad had planned this trip and I wanted it to go well. It wasn't like we saw him much since the divorce. Amy and I lived with Mom in the suburbs. Dad had moved to the city for work. We saw him maybe two weekends a month. But now we would have three days together on a tiny boat . . . with Cory.

The back section of the *Sparta* had a large steering wheel and built-in storage benches around three sides. They were all padlocked. I stepped onto a bench, then onto the deck. The boat swayed back and forth.

Each side bench was wide enough for two people to sit side by side. You'd have to have short legs, or you'd bump knees with the people across the boat. Two could sit on the back bench. Maybe. If nobody was standing at the wheel.

I tugged at the wheel, just to see. It felt greasy. I wiped my hand on my shorts.

There was a cabin below where we would all sleep,

but from what I could see, it looked tiny down there. Five people were going to spend three days on this?

There was no sign of Skipper Jack. He was the man whose picture was on the website. "Hello?" I called.

"Tanner!" Dad said, finally reaching us. "You don't board a skipper's boat – "

"Without asking," came a growly voice from down in the cabin.

I jumped.

A leather-skinned man appeared from the opening that led into the ship's belly. Like the *Sparta*, he looked a good ten or twenty years older than the photo on his website. The man peered up at me.

"Skipper Jack?" I asked. "I'm Tanner Wade. That's my dad and my sister. . . ." I left out Cory. He was still on the dock. "We're here for our trip to the Bahamas."

The old man shook his head. "Didn't you get my message? It's gonna storm, for sure. We ain't going out today."

I looked up at the perfectly blue sky, then back at the captain. "Are you serious?"

He crossed his arms over his broad chest. "Aye."

I crossed my arms, too, and stepped closer. Dad had been excited about this trip. It meant a lot to him, so I didn't want it to fall through.

"I checked the forecast," I told him. "They're calling for perfect sailing weather." What was this old guy trying to do?

Skipper Jack glared at me for a few seconds, then gave a loud "Ha!"

I stepped back.

He leaned forward. "I'm kidding with you, boy. It's a gorgeous day." He clapped his hands together. "Let's sail."

That's what he said. But I caught him looking up at the sky like he didn't quite trust it.

Chapter 2
Puke-Worthy

Five hours later, I was wishing I'd never set foot on the *Sparta*. I'd have jumped off and swum for shore, if I could see it. If I even knew which way it was. But I didn't.

My head was pounding. Amy was seasick. Dad was grouchy. Cory was just Cory.

Only Skipper Jack was in a good mood. He was at the wheel of his boat and the sails were full. The big sail was called the main, I knew, and Dad called the little front one the jib. I could walk around on top of the boat, behind the little guardrail. Up in front, by the jib, my head felt a little better.

"Check on your sister," Dad yelled from the deck.

The wind carried his words to me.

Cory and Amy were down in the cabin, out of the wind. I'd been down there and lasted about two minutes. It was hot and stuffy. Since the waves had gotten big, Amy had spent most of her time in the bathroom, throwing up. The bathroom – the "head" is what Skipper Jack called it – was tiny. Amy had to kneel in the hall and lean over the side of the toilet, with the door wide open. Talk about gross.

Dad said she'd get her sea legs soon. I didn't think it was her legs that were the problem.

I made my way back to the deck and stepped down onto the bench. "Do I have to?"

Dad gave me The Look.

The way into the cabin was through a small door and down a short wooden ladder. The ladder led to the top of a square wooden box. Dad had said the boat's motor was hidden beneath it. From the top of the box, I stepped down onto a stool, and then onto the cabin floor.

After the bright sunlight on deck, the cabin seemed as dark as a cave. Amy was lying on one of the seat benches that ran along the sides. The cushions had worn through in spots and showed their foam rubber

insides. There were three of these: two in the main part of the cabin and one tucked away under the deck. Apparently they were going to be our beds.

We'd take turns, Dad said. I could only shake my head.

The Skipper's bed, of course, was the big one in the very front of the cabin. It was under the front of the boat and actually looked pretty good. At least none of the foam rubber was sticking out.

Amy had taken off her glasses. I wasn't used to seeing her without them. "You okay, kiddo?" I asked her.

She looked at me and groaned. "I hate boats."

I nodded. "I hear you."

The smell of vomit hung in the air. I didn't know how Cory could stand it.

The Slug was lying on the bench bed under the deck. He was as far from Amy as he could get. His knees were bent up a little since he was too tall for the bed. I opened my mouth to say hello, then closed it again. He had his MP3 player going, his earbuds in and his eyes closed. We might as well not have been there.

The ship lurched over a big wave. I braced my hand against the wall to keep from falling. The wood felt sticky. Like spilled Coke . . . or worse. Gross.

Amy rolled off the bench and half-ran, half-stumbled to the bathroom. From the sound of things, she got there just in time. I made a face.

"Little Sis still puking?"

My head snapped up. I didn't much like Cory calling Amy little sis. She wasn't his sister and she wasn't that little, not anymore.

"What's it to you?" I asked.

Cory was sitting up on the end of his bench. He shrugged. "Doesn't bother me. Kind of sums up how I feel about this whole thing." He waved his hand in the air. "Puke-worthy."

Nice attitude. Maybe *Cory* was puke-worthy.

"I'll tell her you were worried about her," I said. I sat down on the bench across from where Amy had been.

He shrugged. "Don't bother. We'll all be out of each other's way soon."

"What's that supposed to mean?" I asked.

"Mom never goes out with any guy for more than a year," Cory said. "Your dad's time is nearly up. I won't miss him."

There was a lot I could have said. That we wouldn't miss Cory, either. That he was wrong about Dad being on his way out. That if Dad got his way, Cory and I would be Stepbrothers!

Talk about puke-worthy. I stared at the dirty carpet. Amy made a retching sound. Poor kid.

"Didn't you hear me?" Cory asked.

"What's your problem, Cory?" I asked, standing. "So your mom gets around. I wouldn't brag about that if I were you." I felt a rush, saying it. I'd won.

But the feeling didn't last. The truth was, Cory's mother was cool. I liked her, mostly. She made Dad smile. But her son was a jerk.

"Don't talk about my mom!" Cory shouted.

He jumped up and ran at me. There was no room to dodge, but the boat tilted and Cory stumbled forward. He slammed his head against a cupboard, then dropped down onto Amy's bench.

"Look . . ." I began. I never worked out what I was going to say. I never got the chance.

Dad opened the cabin door and stared down at us. The light coming through the opening behind him was a weird greenish color. He threw us three sets of straps and three life jackets, the keyhole kind. Faded red cotton. "Boys, put these on. Harness first, then life jacket. Like this."

Dad wasn't wearing a life jacket, only a harness. It wrapped around his chest and came down over his shoulders in a V with a metal clip in front. "Tanner, help your sister with hers. We've got a problem."

Chapter 3

Outrun the Storm

I struggled with my harness and then tugged on a life jacket. The thing smelled musty and old. Did it even float?

Amy was puking. I gave her a minute to catch her breath, then helped her put on her harness. Cory, of course, had snatched the only decent life jacket.

Once Amy was taken care of, I stepped up onto the engine box to see out on deck. In minutes, everything had changed. Wind whipped at my face and howled in my ears. Dad's jacket ballooned out behind him. Skipper Jack was at the wheel, shouting orders, while Dad ran around and pulled ropes. I'd never seen Dad on a boat before. It made me feel good that he seemed to know what he was doing.

But it was the sky that really scared me. The sky was a sickly gray-green color. And the waves had grown big. Instead of rocking over them, the *Sparta* was crashing from one to the other. The ship would rise up and then come banging down. Water splashed over the railings.

"What's going on?" Amy asked. She was behind me. I tried to use my body to block the opening and keep her down below, but she kept pushing me, like she had to see. I climbed the last two steps onto the deck.

There was nothing but ocean and storm all around. I could see the rain coming toward us. It raced across the water, a dark shadow. I hoped the Skipper had one heck of an engine hidden under that wooden box.

"Reef the main," Skipper Jack yelled. The words meant nothing to me. But when Dad loosened a rope, the main sail started sliding down its mast. Up close, the sail was all covered in dark specks.

Dad started gathering it into a large, messy bundle. I tried to help but Dad shook his head. "Get down below, Tanner. Look after your sister."

I studied my dad's face. The first raindrops spattered down, making it look like my dad was crying.

Dad met my eyes. "Go on," he said.

I climbed down the ladder. A minute later, Dad was sliding boards into place across the door to the cabin.

"Don't," I said, as he started to slide the final board across.

Dad looked down and smiled at me. "It'll be all right." And then he pushed the board into place.

It was just the three of us now, me and Amy and Cory, down in that dark, little cabin. Cory sat on one of the benches, hunched up. Amy gripped a small table to keep her balance. I found a handle on the wall to hold onto as our ship lurched over waves.

Then there was a sound, a coughing from below us. Another cough or two, and then a dull roar. The *Sparta* shook as her engine started up. The floorboards buzzed under my feet.

Then we hit rougher seas. We rose up higher than before and then dropped so fast that my stomach was left behind. It was like being on a roller coaster. Amy stumbled for the toilet again. Cory looked green, and I wasn't feeling so great myself. It had been better with the door open. The wind and rain had helped.

I stood and braced myself against a wall. Standing made me feel more in control. Cory pulled some pills out of his pocket. He shook two into his hand.

"What's that?" I asked.

"Gravol," he said.

Gravol. The pills that keep you from throwing up. My face grew hot. "You had Gravol this whole time and you didn't tell us? With my sister puking her guts out ten feet away from you?"

He swallowed the pills. "If she wanted some, she should have brought her own."

I made my way over to him step by step, fighting the rocking and pounding of the boat. "Give me the pills."

"They're mine."

Cory was bigger than me, both taller and wider. But I'd fight him if I had to. "You're a jerk, you know that? But if you were sick and Amy had the Gravol, she'd share. Even though you're a – "

Cory held up a hand to stop me. He sniffed the air. "Something's burning."

"What?" Had Cory even heard me? Was this some kind of joke?

But then I smelled it, too. Smoke, and a smell like

too-hot metal or melting plastic. I turned to the mini-kitchen tucked against one side of the boat. The stove wasn't on. The problem wasn't out there – it was under our feet.

Dark, oily smoke was streaming from the engine box.

Chapter 4

Engine Fire

The smoke was coming from under the box. It was leaking out around the edges.

I touched the box. Hot. I snatched my hand away. I reached back for a dishcloth I'd seen in the sink and wrapped it around my fingers.

The front-facing part of the box looked like it could slide up and down. A panel. There was a lip along the top of the panel. A crack ran between the panel and the rest of the box, and smoke was oozing out of there, too.

I tugged at the panel. There was a step attached to it. It was all solid wood, so it weighed a ton.

"Help me," I shouted at Cory.

Cory hung back. "Do you know what you're doing?"

"We have to see what's going on," I said. I tugged again. This time Cory helped me lift the thing. As we raised the panel, dark smoke poured into the cabin. I coughed and choked.

"What the – " Cory started. His words gave way to a coughing fit.

I slammed the panel back down. "Dad!" I yelled.

Smoke was still leaking out around the engine box. I didn't want to stand on it. Instead, I climbed up on the storage cabinet beside it. Then I banged on the boards across the opening.

"Fire! The engine's on fire!" I shouted.

The *Sparta* kept roller-coastering over waves. I grabbed a shelf to keep from falling. I banged the boards again. Could anybody hear me over the storm?

"Get down low," I shouted to Cory and Amy. Smoke rises. But this smoke seemed heavy. Greasy. "Dad! Skipper! The engine's on fire!" My voice cracked. I hacked and coughed.

Flames began licking at the top surface of the box from around the edges. We were trapped below the deck. Smoke was coming up from below. I broke into a sweat. How long did we have? Minutes?

"Open the thing," Amy yelled. She was holding a fire extinguisher, aimed at the box over the engine.

I grabbed the dishcloth again, wrapped it around my hands and lifted. The panel was too heavy. I bent my knees and tried again. The panel slid free.

Heat singed my leg hairs. I was standing too close to the flames.

Amy pulled the pin from the fire extinguisher. She squeezed the handle. White spray hissed out of the extinguisher and sizzled when it landed. The smoke got worse.

Amy swept the extinguisher back and forth. She managed to hit the fire most of the time. But then, way too soon, the white spray dribbled to a stop. There was a sputtering sound, the sound a straw makes trying to suck water from the bottom of a glass. I grabbed the extinguisher from her and pulled the nozzle myself, but it only hissed.

No spray.

But there were still flames. And smoke. So much smoke that my eyes watered. "Get back," I choked, hoping Amy heard me.

I bent at the waist, then fell to my knees, hunching forward. I was way too close to the fire. My face wanted to crack from the heat of it. But I could see the engine. It wasn't moving anymore. Small puddles of oil or gas were forming on the floor beside the engine. Blue flames danced on them. And then I felt a weight on my back. Someone stepped on me – someone heavy, whose foot pressed right between my shoulder blades.

Cory. It had to be. His weight crushed me, and then lifted. I looked up. There was light, and the smoke was being drawn upward. The boards were gone. So was the weight on my back.

I peered around the smoky cabin for Amy. Flames were spreading along the top of the engine box, licking at the wall. I grabbed a pillow off one of the beds and beat at the flames. "Amy!"

Dad jumped down into the cabin and helped me put out the fire that we could reach. He was wearing a life jacket and harness like we were. His windbreaker was tied around his waist. The Skipper was right behind him.

No one was steering the boat. With no sails and no motor, we were at the mercy of the ocean.

Dad crushed me into a hug. "Are you all right?"

"Where's Amy?" I asked. My throat was raw.

I felt her hands on my arm. "I'm here," she said. "We have to get out of here."

Skipper Jack looked down at the motor and swore. "We're taking on water."

Dad's body tensed. "Up top, both of you. I want all three of you in the lifeboat, ready to go." There was a small, hard-shelled rowboat fastened across the back of the *Sparta*, like a tiny shell on a giant turtle. Was that what he meant? The lifeboat wouldn't last five seconds in these waves. But the flames and the smoke were spreading. I nodded.

Dad lifted Amy out of the cabin. Skipper Jack flicked some buttons on a radio that was attached to the wall. "Mayday, mayday," he shouted. And then Dad crouched down for me. He put his hands together for me to step on, and boosted me up into clean air.

Chapter 5

Angry Waves

Amy and Cory were on deck, clinging to the ship's steering wheel. Cory had his eyes squeezed shut. Amy shouted something at me, but the wind stole her words. Smoke was still pouring up out of the cabin.

The *Sparta*, our boat, had turned sideways to the waves. Now the waves crashed over the left railing. The water came washing over the deck where we stood. The boat tossed back and forth like crazy. I didn't know what was keeping the *Sparta* upright. Skipper Jack had said we were taking on water. Did that mean we were going to sink?

Dad climbed up behind me. He clipped a rope to each of our harnesses. Then he fastened the other end of the rope to the railing at the edge of the boat. "Just in case," he said. He winked as if he were joking, but his fingers were shaking. Then he untied his jacket from around his waist and made Amy put it on.

Dad worked his way up onto the front of the boat. His own safety line was clipped to the taller, wire railing that led around the top part of the boat. It was held up by a set of metal poles. When Dad came to a pole, he unclipped the line and re-clipped it on the other side. Each time he did that, I held my breath. Once, he slipped when a wave washed over his feet. I reached for him. Stupid. It was like reaching to catch someone in a movie. My fingers closed on air.

Dad fell, but he grabbed the pole and clipped himself to it. He stayed there, just holding on, and then slowly got to his feet.

Amy was watching Dad, too. Her face was white.

"I'm going to help," I said.

She nodded.

I worked my way along the top of the boat just like Dad had done. Each time I had to re-clip my safety line, each time my foot slipped as a wave washed over, my heart sped up.

When Dad saw me coming, he shouted something.

I knew by his face that it wasn't good. The wind drowned out his words, so I pretended he might have said, "Come help."

Dad worked his way up onto the top, near where the mast joined the boat. There was a white box there, about the size of a suitcase. It was attached to the deck with some kind of metal frame. Dad started wrestling with it, trying to get the box out of the frame. He needed two hands to grab it, though. With only one free hand, he was getting nowhere.

I worked my way to his side. I saw the straps that held the box into the metal frame. Together, we worked them free. Dad clipped a rope onto the box and then threw it over the side of the ship. The box opened up as it flew. All the folded-up plastic inside began puffing up and sticking out in strange directions. It was like watching a hot air balloon unfold itself. I couldn't tear my eyes away.

Thirty seconds later, a fully formed life raft floated on the waves. It was held to the *Sparta* by a rope, and the rope was pulled tight by the waves. It looked as though the life raft – a giant, six-sided inner tube – wanted to escape on its own.

"You'll have to swim for it, Tanner," Dad shouted

over the wind. "We'll fasten you to the guide line so you can't drift off. You and Amy go together, so you can help her."

I nodded. A rope ladder hung down one side of the raft. There were a lot of angry waves between me and that ladder.

Dad worked his way back to Cory and Amy. Waves and wind kept trying to pull me off the boat. I clung to one of the wires that led up to the top of the mast.

It seemed to take forever before the three of them made it to where I was. Amy was crying. "I don't want to," she told Dad. "You have to come too."

Dad gave her a hug. "I'm going to help the Skipper. If we can make the boat safe, we will. If not, I'll join you."

"Promise," Amy said.

He kissed her on top of her head. "I promise. Now come on. You first, Tanner."

But Cory had already shoved past us. He clipped his line to the rope that led to the floating raft. Before Dad could say a word, Cory jumped off the *Sparta* and into the water.

For about half a second, I admired Cory's bravery. Then I figured out why he jumped. He thought he was better off in the raft than on the *Sparta*. He was just looking out for himself.

"Dad – " I started. The boat rocked to one side. We both staggered.

"Go," Dad ordered. "Look after your sister."

"Come fast," I said. "–

"I'll see you soon," he promised. He clipped both of our safety lines to the rope, and to each other's. Then he double checked by tugging on them.

Amy tucked her glasses under her shirt. I grabbed her hand. We jumped together into the rolling sea.

Chapter 6

A Leaf in a Tornado

I fell hard into the water. It was shockingly warm. I started to say so to Amy when a wave hit me.

The wave ripped me away from Amy. I was like a leaf in a tornado, rushing out of control. The water swirled around me, over me, dragging me . . . and then, suddenly, I felt a yank on my safety harness. I stopped short. The line held.

Amy had managed to grab hold of the rope to the raft. She was halfway between the raft and the *Sparta*, clinging to it, screaming. The waves kept crashing over her. At least I knew that the safety line would hold, if she lost her grip.

I pulled myself along my safety line, hand over

hand, back to the main rope. My life jacket kept me afloat, but it didn't keep the waves from trying to knock me down. They surged against my face, filling my mouth and nose. I coughed and spat as I inched along the line.

Finally I reached Amy. "Got you," I said, putting my hands over hers on the rope. She kicked frantically underwater. Her foot caught me in the knee. "Amy! Stop it. You have to – " a wave broke over us. I clung to Amy. She kept fighting me. "Calm down!"

"Dad," she said, looking back at the *Sparta*.

Neither of us could see him. All we could see was the *Sparta*, waves crashing over it. The boat was much lower in the back than in the front. It reminded me of that *Titanic* movie, where the ship stands almost straight up before taking her final dive.

I swallowed. Now was not the time to think about the *Titanic*.

"He's coming," I said. "We have to – " another wave. " – Get to the raft."

Cory was already climbing into the raft. He hauled himself over the edge and fell inside. Now he was safe and we were still in the water.

I could only grit my teeth.

Amy clung to my back like a little kid. We swam together, slowly, holding onto the rope that led to the raft. I learned to push down and kick when the waves hit. "Good," I told Amy. "Almost there." Saying it made me feel better.

When we reached the life raft, I was panting. My life jacket and harness made a tight band around my ribs. I wanted to rip them off so I could breathe. But not now. They'd kept us alive so far and might have to do it again.

The life raft was rubbery on the bottom, nylon on top. It was slick with water, too slick to climb up. But a sort of rope ladder made of webbing hung down one side.

"Can you climb?" I asked Amy.

She nodded. I helped Amy to get her foot onto the ladder, but her legs shook so hard she couldn't push herself up.

"Cory!" I shouted. "Help! Pull her up!"

He cowered on the far side of the raft. Was he afraid we'd tip it?

A wave knocked Amy off the ladder. I grabbed her life jacket and pulled her back. "Come on," I said. We stuck our feet in the bottom loop of the ladder together.

I helped her climb, staying just behind and below her.

There were only three rungs, but they sank when we stepped on them. It was hard to climb and fight the waves at the same time. One rung. Up. Another rung. Push. Another. . . .

Finally, Amy got her rib cage over the top of the raft. She kicked and rolled her way into the lifeboat. Her heel banged my jaw.

Spots blinked in front of my eyes. I pressed my hand to my jaw and clung to the raft.

"Tanner!" Amy called from above me. At least she was safe. She grabbed at my life jacket and tugged. She was trying to pull me up, but I was too heavy.

"Wait," I said. "Give me a minute." I took a breath. Then I hauled myself onto the last rung.

When I reached the top, Amy was there, yanking at my life jacket until I tumbled into the raft.

I lay there, stunned. The three of us were safe, at least for now. The three of us had escaped the sinking boat. But what about Dad? I struggled to my knees and looked for him.

The *Sparta*'s front end was barely above water now. Smoke still poured from the cabin. I didn't see Dad or the Skipper.

"We have to get to them," I shouted. I started pulling on the rope that attached us to the *Sparta*. Hand over hand, fighting the waves, I tried to pull us back there.

When I felt Cory's shoulder against mine, I thought he was going to help. I let him grab the rope. That was my mistake.

Cory unclipped it from the raft. My white-knuckled grip on the rope was the only thing holding us to the *Sparta*.

"What are you doing?" I shouted.

"That boat's sinking!" he yelled. "It'll pull us down, too!"

"My Dad is on that boat!" I started to pull again, hand over hand.

Amy tackled Cory, scratching him and pulling his hair. He batted at her.

Meanwhile, I was being pulled out of the life raft. The top of it was wet and slippery, and the tug of the waves against the *Sparta*'s rope was too much. From the waist up, I hung out over the water. I hooked my foot through a strap to try and hold on to both the raft and the rope. But I was being pulled into two pieces.

"Tanner, you can't!" Amy yelled. She grabbed my legs and tugged me back. It took a split second, no more. I lost my grip. The rope was gone. The *Sparta* plunged into the storm.

Chapter 7

The Sparta *is Lost*

I stared into the storm. With each gust of wind, we pulled away from the sinking *Sparta*. With each wave, she grew smaller.

"Dad!" I screamed, cupping my hands around my mouth. The wind carried my voice away.

I didn't realize I was standing until Amy tugged at my wrist. "Get down!"

But I didn't. I couldn't. Two tiny figures appeared on the deck of the *Sparta*. I couldn't see what they were doing. One of them pointed our way. I waved my arms back and forth. How could we get back there?

Then I had an idea. "There have to be paddles in this thing!" I shouted. "Get me the paddles."

Amy held up an aluminum paddle. It was no bigger than the plastic ones on a child's blow-up boat. I stared at it. "The other's broken," she said.

I grabbed the good paddle from her. I knelt at the side of the raft, leaned over, and started paddling.

It was worse than useless. The waves pushed us where they wanted. And the waves didn't want us back with the *Sparta*.

I screamed and threw the tiny paddle out to sea. Then I panicked and tried to reach it.

"Moron!" Cory grabbed me by the shoulders and pulled me back to the center of the raft. "What did you do that for?"

"My Dad's on that boat," I said. I felt like someone had punched a hole in me and let all the air out. My voice was small and my eyes burned.

"And there's nothing we can do about it," Cory said.

I shook him off and knelt in the middle of the raft. The *Sparta* was a speck now, a small speck on a big ocean. I stared and stared. As long as I kept her in sight, Dad and I were connected.

But I was too weak. I blinked.

The *Sparta* disappeared.

Chapter 8

Two Packets of Water

I knelt there for a long time. I kept staring at the spot on the waves where the *Sparta* had disappeared. Now there was nothing. Nothing.

Slowly, I noticed things again. The rubber smell of the raft. Salt drying, itchy, on my skin. The springy feel of the inflated floor beneath my knees. Amy and Cory were moving around, opening things, talking in low voices.

The storm had passed. The wind had died down, and the sun was bright again. The sea was smooth, like rippled glass. It was as if everything was fine. As if we were out here for fun.

Unreal.

"Tanner?" It was Amy. She had her glasses on again.

I turned. She and Cory had taken off their life jackets and safety harnesses. Amy wore Dad's windbreaker tied around her waist. I swallowed.

"Here." Amy held out a soda cracker. "You should eat something. And take off your life jacket. The storm's over."

I took the cracker.

Cory stared at me. Amy was watching me, too. So I swallowed the last bit of the cracker. It was dry and salty and the last thing I wanted.

"There isn't much on this boat, but we have a few supplies," Amy said.

"What – what supplies?" I asked. It was the first thing I'd said that wasn't a scream. The words came out rusty and broken.

Amy brightened. "Here," she said. She showed me two pouches that had been attached to the inside of the life raft. One read First Aid; the other, Rations. There was also a metal box labeled Supplies. Inside it, we found just a few things. There was a waterproof flashlight with weak batteries. Packed beside it were a compass, a whistle, and some coiled-up fishing line.

Then there was a small mirror. Who put a mirror in a safety kit?

I held it up. "In case we need to fix our hair?"

"For signaling," Amy said. She took the mirror from me and flashed a beam of sunlight into my eyes.

I blocked the light with my arm. "Put that thing away."

When my eyes stopped watering, she showed me the rest of the stuff. The rations pouch held about a dozen packages of soda crackers, mostly crumbled. There were two granola bars with ancient wrappers. And some pills. Vitamin C, the label read.

"Water?" I asked.

Amy's face fell. "A little," she told me. "There were three packets. Two good ones. One of them must have burst when it was still inside the suitcase." She held up an empty, clear plastic tube. It was about the size of a small carton of milk. So we had maybe a litre of water. For all three of us.

Cory cleared his throat.

I didn't wait for him to make an excuse. "I don't want to hear anything you have to say. Got it?"

"Tanner . . ." Amy started.

"No," I said. "Cory unclipped the rope. He's the reason Dad . . ."

I couldn't say it.

Amy squeezed her eyes shut. Her shoulders shook, and her face turned red. She curled her hands into tight fists and crossed her arms in front of her face.

I touched her shoulder, but she jerked away.

"Don't," she said.

"Amy. . . ."

She shook her head, blinking back tears.

I looked at the endless ocean. At our tiny, ruined paddle, crumbling around the edge. At the empty sky above. We had nothing but time.

"If you need to cry, you cry," I finally told her. It's what Dad would have said. Then I hugged her, and she rested her head on my shoulder.

After a few seconds, she sat up and sniffed. "No," she said. "He might still be okay."

I had no answer for that. "Let's go through the first aid pouch," I said. It would take our thoughts off . . . other things.

"Cory and I already did," she said. "He helped me fix my leg."

That got my attention. "What's wrong with your leg?"

She pulled up her shorts just a little to show a white

bandage wrapped around her thigh. "I gashed it on something getting off the boat," she said. "It's not that bad. Just a big cut." She held her fingers about three inches apart.

Not bad as long as it didn't get infected. I whipped around to face Cory. "Did you clean it?"

"With what?" He held his hands wide apart. "There's almost nothing in that kit. Aspirin and a little foil blanket and some Band-aids. It's useless. What kind of a life raft is this, anyhow?" He threw the words at me like it was my fault.

"Oh, I don't know." I crossed my arms. "The kind that saved our lives?"

Cory leaned forward, jabbing his finger into my face. "Back off, Mr. Perfect. Amy and I checked out the raft while you sat there like a lump. And I fixed your sister's leg, as best I could. What else do you want?"

What did I want? I wanted Dad back, but the words dried up on my tongue. Cory had bandaged Amy's leg, and I hadn't even seen it. I'd let myself get lost in my own world. But Amy was my sister, not his. She was my responsibility. *Look after her*, that was what Dad had said.

"Sorry," I replied. The word tasted like chalk. I

looked down at my feet. "Now what?" I asked. Maybe it was okay to admit that I didn't know what to do next. Maybe Cory or Amy would have an idea.

"Now we wait," Cory said, leaning into a corner of the raft. Amy had already curled up against one of the sides. It looked like she was trying to sleep. She had a life jacket for a pillow.

I stared into the empty sky again and shielded my eyes against the sun.

It might be a long wait.

Chapter 9

Stupid Slug

I woke up with the sun in my eyes and a rotten taste in my mouth. It took me a few blinks to remember where I was. I sat up slowly and looked around. The sun hung low in the sky. A cool breeze blew. Sunset, and we were all alone. A tiny dot on the giant ocean.

Amy and Cory were both asleep. Cory was sprawled against one of the six corners of the raft, snoring. His head hung back. His legs reached more than halfway across the raft.

Amy was curled on her side against another wall. She seemed to be tucked into the shadows.

I tried to say something to her, but my voice didn't work. My throat felt dry and achy. Like sandpaper. I hadn't had a drink in hours. Now I could feel it.

I'd never been so thirsty.

But we only had two packets of water between the three of us. How long would they last? How many drinks could any of us take before all the water was gone?

Our supplies were scattered around the raft. We'd need to do something about that. We couldn't afford to lose any more if another storm came up.

I wanted to take one drink of water. Just one. So I felt around looking for the water packets. I wasn't about to open one without talking to Amy and Cory. It seemed like something we should decide together. But there was no harm in just finding them, was there?

I bumped Cory's leg. He sat up suddenly. "Who's there?"

"Sorry," I said. The word didn't taste like chalk this time. "I'm looking for the water. Have you – oh." His face and neck were bright, pinkish red. Now that I looked, his arms and legs were sunburned, too.

"What?" he asked.

I gulped. There wasn't much we could do about sunburn, and I didn't want him upset. But somebody had to tell him. "You might have had too much sun," I said.

He pressed an outspread hand against his leg, just above the knee. It left a white handprint. As the blood flowed back, it turned red again. He swore. "Why didn't you wake me up?"

Why was everything my fault?

"I fell asleep too, all right?"

Cory swore again. "You mean there might have been a boat or a plane come by, and we missed it? None of us was awake to do anything about it?"

The truth hit me like a punch to the gut. He was right, but I didn't want to admit it. "We'd have heard," I said. I hoped it was true. "From now on, we'll sleep in shifts."

Cory grunted and turned his back to the sun. Not that it mattered now. The sky was already glowing orange and pink.

"Do you know where the water is?" I asked.

Cory felt around behind him and came out with a sealed package.

"There were two," I said.

"I drank the other one," he said.

"You what?" It wasn't a shout. It wasn't even loud. My voice was steady and cold with anger. "Cory. What did you do?"

Behind me, I heard Amy sit up.

"You guys were sleeping and I was thirsty," Cory said. "Once I opened it, what was I supposed to do? I couldn't exactly set it down. It would have spilled. What's the big deal?"

"We had two packets of water to last until rescue comes," I said. "You just cut our water supply in half."

Amy took in a sharp breath.

"There's water all around us!" Cory said. "What's

your problem? It's salty, but it can't be that bad."

"How stupid are you?" Amy asked. "You can't drink salt water . . . you'd die."

"Well, we could. . . ." Cory's words dropped off. We could what?

My head was pounding. We couldn't afford to fight. "Stop it," I said. "Just stop, okay? It's done. You drank the water and it's gone. Now I need to work out what to do next."

"You? Who made you the leader?" Cory asked.

"Maybe because he's smart enough not to drink all our water!" Amy shouted. "Stupid Slug!"

I filled my lungs. "Enough!"

They both jumped.

Amy stared at me with wide eyes. Her chin was trembling. "You sounded just like – "

Like Dad. I sounded like Dad. I took another deep breath, but this time, it wasn't for shouting. "I think we need to open the second packet," I said. "Amy and I will have a small drink, then we'll pour the rest into the metal box and put it somewhere safe. Cory, you've had your share for today. Starting tomorrow, we share it evenly and try to make it last. One sip at a time, that's all."

"What about food?" Cory sounded cold, but at least he didn't argue about the water. "I'm hungry."

I looked over our supplies. As the sun sank, the air grew colder and colder. Amy put Dad's windbreaker on properly. "We'll share one of the granola bars," I said.

Amy nodded. "It'll give us some energy for staying warm tonight." She broke up the granola bar. She did a pretty good job of making the pieces even, but the piece she gave me was a little bigger than the one she gave Cory. I didn't complain.

"They'll probably find us in the morning," Cory said, looking at his tiny piece of granola bar.

I didn't bother to answer. Maybe they would. Maybe not. We had to be ready either way.

By the time we finished our bit of the granola bar, the sun was down. Darkness fell fast. We agreed that I'd take first watch. When I couldn't stay awake anymore, I'd wake up Cory. Amy would go last, toward morning. Nobody would use the flashlight except for giving a signal to a boat or plane.

Cory and Amy both dropped off pretty quickly, despite having slept all afternoon. Cory's sunburn must have been rough for him. If he hadn't drunk half the water, I might have felt sorry for him.

Amy shivered in her sleep. I dug the folded foil blanket out of the first aid kit and tucked it around her. It was a clear night, and the moon reflected off the shiny foil. It made her look like a baked potato.

I hugged my legs close to my body for warmth.

I started to think about Dad, then stopped myself. Instead, I looked up at the night sky. There were more stars than I'd ever seen in my life, but they were too far away to help us. I'd have traded every last one of them for a rescue plane.

Chapter 10

Fishing for Seaweed

Our second day at sea. It was midmorning, and the day was growing hotter by the second. As the sun climbed, there was less and less shade for us to hide in. Cory had tried ducking under the tin foil blanket, but he said it was like being in an oven. Amy made him try Dad's windbreaker, but that didn't help. Cory was so sunburned that nothing would help.

We'd each had two mouthfuls of water, but the level in the can had gone down too much already. What happened when we ran out?

"Look out there!" Amy shouted. She was pointing at something, out on the water.

I shielded my eyes and tried to see why Amy was so excited. All I saw were waves.

"I don't see anything," I admitted. And maybe she was seeing things.

Cory peered over the edge of the raft. "That dark thing?" he asked.

Amy nodded. "I think it's seaweed!"

"Seaweed on the ocean," Cory said. "Great."

I agreed with Cory, but I wouldn't have told him that. We had bigger things to worry about than seaweed.

Amy folded her arms across the edge of the raft. She stared out at the endless blue. "It's coming closer," she said.

Cory rolled his eyes. "It's a seaweed monster. Watch out."

"For your information, Cory, seaweed makes good insulation," Amy said. "And there are lots of kinds you can eat."

She caught my interest. I sat up, ignoring the stiffness of my clothes and skin. "How do you know so much about seaweed?"

"Survival badge," Amy said smugly.

Cory snorted. "Seaweed badge."

"No, seriously," I said. "It got cold last night. If we

can use this stuff for insulation, we should grab it."
I wasn't sure about eating the seaweed. If I got any hungrier, though, I might be willing to try.

"Grab it with what?" Cory asked.

Amy held up the lousy paddle. Some of the blade had crumbled away, but the stick part was fine.

I nodded. "If the seaweed gets close enough. We're not swimming for it."

"Or . . ." Amy said. She seemed to be thinking about something.

"Or what?" I asked.

"Or we could fish for it." She picked up one of the safety lines. "What do you think?"

It took a bit of work, but we finally had it. "It" was about twenty feet of rope attached to one of the life jackets. At the end, another foot of rope with a large hook hung down from the life jacket. We broke one of the safety clips to make the hook.

Amy named it the seaweed catcher.

I tried it first. I knelt beside one edge of the raft and swung the seaweed catcher around over my head. It was like a lasso.

"Hey!" Cory shouted. The hook had just missed him.

"You guys have to duck," I said. I tried again. Three swings around and then I let go of the rope.

The seaweed catcher sailed out over the waves and landed with a plop about eight feet from our raft. Not far enough to catch any seaweed.

"Let me try," Cory said.

I wanted to be the one to bring in the seaweed, but I handed him the rope. "If you miss, I get the next throw," I said.

"Hello?" Amy said. "What about me?"

Cory and I looked at each other and shrugged.

Amy and I ducked while Cory swung the life jacket over his head. It made a whooshing noise when he did it. That hadn't happened for me.

He let go. The life jacket flew in a perfect arc and landed right on top of the seaweed.

"Nice," I said. I ignored the bitter taste in my mouth.

Amy got to haul it in, because she hadn't had the chance to throw it. Some of the seaweed broke away, but most of it came right to us.

It was a big, tangled mess. There was even a piece of wood caught in it, almost as long as my outstretched arms. It looked like it had come from a two-by-four.

The wood wasn't waterlogged yet. Had it come from the *Sparta*? The thought gave me a funny feeling in the pit of my stomach.

While I got the two-by-four, Amy and Cory hauled in armful after armful of damp, stinky seaweed. "Great catch," I said. If we didn't get rescued soon, they'd be able to find us by our smell.

"At least we'll be warmer tonight," Amy said, grinning. "And it gives us some sun protection during the day."

"This stuff is gross," Cory said, spitting a mouthful of green stuff over the side.

"Cory, no!" Amy yelled.

"What?" He spat again. "You said it was edible."

"Only some kinds," Amy said, staring at Cory. "Some kinds can . . . can make you sick."

Cory sank down in the raft, one hand on his stomach. Beneath his sunburn, he'd gone pale. "How sick?"

"I don't know," Amy said. But she bit her lip. She only bit her lip when she was lying.

"Did you swallow any?" I asked.

He shook his head.

"That's good," Amy said. "Probably." She didn't sound sure.

I looked around at the armloads of seaweed in the raft. It was stinky and slimy and full of bugs. When it dried, it would crumble and make our skin itch.

"My lips feel numb," Cory said. His hands shook.

I moved closer to him and handed him the water box. "Rinse your mouth out," I said. I didn't know what else to do for him.

His eyes met mine over the top of the box. He took a sip.

And then Cory threw up over the edge of the raft.

Chapter 11

Get the Mirror!

Cory spent the next half hour puking over the side of the raft. Not really puking, I guess. There wasn't much to come out, but his stomach kept trying. He pulled the Gravol out of his pocket and tried to get it open, but I took it away. Gravol wouldn't help him.

"I'm not trying to be mean," I said. "Amy says your body needs to get all the stuff from the seaweed out." I hoped she was right. I stuck the Gravol in the first aid pouch with the aspirin and the Band-aids.

When Cory wasn't throwing up, Amy dribbled seawater over his forehead from her cupped hands. It seemed to make him feel better. Of the three of us, he was in the most trouble.

Finally, Cory stopped throwing up. He still wouldn't drink any of the fresh water. Instead, he curled on his side in the bottom of the raft and fell asleep.

The sun beat down on all of us. Amy sat beside me and leaned her head on my shoulder. "Are you thinking of Dad?" she asked.

And I felt bad, because I hadn't been. I hadn't been thinking about anything. "Yeah," I lied.

"Me too," she said. "He'll find us. He'll get us home to Mom."

I didn't answer her. I wanted to believe that she was right, that he was still alive and looking for us. I just didn't see how he could be. And it hurt too much to think about that.

She sat up and looked at me. "What do we do now?"

"I don't know." We needed water. We needed shade. We needed rescue. The stink of seaweed was almost unbearable. I grabbed a fistful and flung it out of the raft. "I hate this stuff."

"Don't," she said. "We'll need it tonight, when it gets cold."

I shrugged. Maybe we'd all be rescued by the time night fell. Maybe we'd be dead. Maybe, maybe, maybe. I punched the raft, but my fist only bounced back. The

worst part was that there was nothing we could do. Just wait.

But . . . maybe there was something. "Amy," I said. "Grab me the fishing line. I've got an idea."

It took most of the afternoon to build our shelter. I did most of the moving around, because Amy's leg was hurting. Even so, I wasn't moving too fast. Between the heat and the lack of water, nobody had much energy left. But we did it.

The sides of the raft were about two feet high, and there were loops on the sides to tie things to. We strung a rope across the middle, nice and tight. Then I ran the safety straps around that rope and back to the loops along one side of the raft. I wove more rope back and forth through the straps. When I finished, it looked like a spider web over half of the boat. Then I took off my t-shirt. Amy helped me tear it down the sides, so I had a front piece and a back piece. We wove those, keeping them as flat as we could, between the ropes and straps.

In the end, we had two t-shirts worth of shade over one half of the boat, and a crawl space about two feet high. We couldn't all fit under there at once, but we could take turns getting out of the sun.

I shook Cory's shoulder, meaning to have him move into the shade.

"Airplane," he croaked, sitting up.

"What?" I stuck a hand on his forehead. He was hot, but then, we were all hot. But Cory looked wrong. All the bones of his face showed, like his skin had sucked closer to them.

"Airplane. I heard it," he said.

I listened. There was a low, buzzing sound in the

air. Amy and I had been so busy building the shelter, we hadn't noticed. We'd forgotten to watch for rescue.

"There!" Amy said, pointing up at the sky. The plane was a distant speck. "Get the signal mirror!"

I scrambled for the mirror. "How do we do this?" The sun was facing the wrong way from the airplane. Did it matter? I held up the mirror and turned it to the sun. I moved it in every direction.

"Blanket," Cory said.

"In a minute," I said.

Cory grabbed my arm. "No! Get the foil blanket."

Amy was ahead of me. She held it up and let the wind spread the blanket wide like a flag.

But the plane kept straight on, flying away from us.

"No!" I shouted. I stood, holding the signal mirror high. The raft rocked under my feet. Amy reached to steady me – and a gust of wind snatched the foil blanket from her.

I grabbed at it. It dodged my fingers. And then I tripped over the rope we'd just strung across the raft for the shelter. I scrambled for balance. Too late. I fell forward, over the side of the raft.

Chapter 12

Like a Giant Fish

I surfaced, spitting salt water. The raft was only a few feet from me. I swam for it. A wave yanked it – or me – away.

Still not too far. The water was warm. I could make it. Then another wave, pushing me one way and the raft another. It was farther now. There was a panicky, squeezing feeling in my chest. Amy was screaming my name.

Cory had the seaweed catcher. He swung it around and around over his head. Then he threw it at me, but another guest of wind took it. The seaweed catcher landed nearby. I swam for it, but the waves pushed it away.

Cory hauled in the seaweed catcher for another try. I shouted at him to leave it. Then I chased after it, but he kept pulling it in. My arms felt heavy. Why was I tired so soon? Why couldn't he just leave it there?

Again, Cory swung the seaweed catcher over his head.

The life jacket came straight for me. But the large metal seaweed hook, that was coming at me too. I ducked to one side, but not enough. The hook clipped me in the forehead. Dizzy, I barely managed to grab the life jacket and hang on.

By the time I reached the raft, the dizziness was gone. But now blood was streaming over my left eye. I could taste it, like metal on my tongue. And I could see a red haze over one eye.

Amy and Cory helped me climb into the raft. I flopped on the floor like a giant fish. Then I remembered the gash in my head. I pressed a hand to my forehead.

Someone – Amy or Cory – put a ripped piece of cloth on the cut.

"Stay still," Amy told me. "Wait for the bleeding to stop."

So I lay there, waiting. The raft smelled of seaweed, rubber and sweat. The seaweed was starting to dry out. Just like I had expected, it itched. Amy, Cory and I were all crowded into half the raft. It was hot and stinky, wet and slippery.

Home sweet home, I thought.

I giggled. I couldn't help it. And then, seconds later, my giggles grew into full-fledged laughter. It was slightly scary, high-pitched laughter. Amy and Cory stared at me, and that only made me laugh harder. I laughed until tears ran down my face.

"Tanner?" Amy asked. She sounded worried. "Tanner, are you all right?"

There was only one thing I could say. "Sailing sucks, Amy. Sailing really sucks."

• • •

It was evening. Amy was sleeping under the shelter, which sagged a bit in the middle now. Cory and I were watching for planes. It was my watch. Cory dozed off and on.

The wind had picked up at sunset. Mostly, the cool air felt good. Every now and then, a gust of wind blew into the shelter like it was a pocket. When that happened, it puffed up like a plastic bag filling with air. Then the raft shot forward until the gust died. The wind might have taken us somewhere . . . if we knew where to go. If we knew where we were.

Amy had fastened gauze over the cut on my forehead. She said the cut wasn't that bad, it just bled a lot. I might even get a cool eyebrow scar out of it.

Amy didn't get off so lightly. When we peeled the

dressing off her leg, the skin looked bad. The gash wasn't what I had imagined at all. Something sharp had dug into her leg and ripped. Now the skin around the cut was all red and swollen.

"Amy . . ." I began. But I didn't know what to say next. The cut looked infected. And if nothing was done, it was going to get worse. Amy was already dehydrated; we all were. If she ended up with a fever, out here on the raft, she'd die. She might die before anybody found us.

"It'll be okay," she told me. "As soon as we get rescued, the doctors will fix it."

I nodded, and then Cory and I did our best to clean it with salt water. Then I spent the rest of the afternoon thinking. We'd been stuck on this life raft for two nights and a day. We'd seen only one plane and no boats in all that time. Our food was gone. Our water was down to two sips. Amy was sick and my head was feeling none too good. How much longer could we stay alive?

At least she was resting now.

Cory broke into my thoughts. "Think she'll be all right?" he asked.

A day ago, I'd have asked why he cared. She wasn't

his sister. But now I was too tired to be angry at him. Too tired to remember how he drank half our water. Too tired to remember what a jerk he was.

"Amy's tough," I said. "She'll make it." I paused. "How about you?" He'd been pretty sick, not that many hours ago.

"I'm tough too," he said. "You?"

I smiled in the darkness. "Yeah," I said. "I'm tough."

I almost believed it.

Chapter 13

Catching the Wind

The storm came in the middle of the night. Amy shook me awake and I crawled out of the shelter. Cory was already outside. It was darker than our first night had been. No stars.

"Lightning," Amy said. "It's coming closer." She was wearing Dad's windbreaker jacket.

Just then the sky lit up. Lightning streaked down from the clouds. It made a jagged line to the water, then it scattered. Darkness followed. And then – one one thousand, two one thousand – the thunder. A great, booming roll of it.

"Two miles away," Cory said. "Three at the most."

"What do we do?" Amy asked.

I shook my head. What could we do? "We wait," I said, thinking fast. "Or we try to outrun it."

"How?" Cory asked, after a long moment.

The wind was blowing more steadily now. If we raised the shelter higher, and if the raft was facing the right way, we might catch the wind. If we were very, very lucky, it might blow us ahead of the storm.

"Life jackets first,' I said. "Then we sail."

Amy's job was to man the sail. She sat in the middle of the raft, and her job was to push up on the center ropes as hard as she could. That would raise the pocket to catch the wind. In the meantime, she tried to pack seaweed into our mess of ropes.

Cory and I tied the broken paddle to the long piece of wood. He fed it through one of the hand-holds on the side of the raft. That was our rudder. We'd use it to steer the raft – as best we could. We both sat at the back to work the rudder. That way, there was less chance of our losing it. Plus, our weight would help keep the wind from driving the nose of the life raft down.

"Ready?" I asked.

"I think so," Amy said. Her voice shook, just a little. Wind gusted over us sideways. For now, she had to hold the front of the shelter down low. We needed to get the raft facing the right direction.

"Cory?"

"Aye aye, Skipper," he said. Maybe he meant it.

"Let's do it." We shoved the rudder into the inky water and tried it. When we pushed the stick right, it spun the raft left. When we pushed the stick left, it spun the raft right. To catch the wind, we needed to spin about a quarter turn left.

It was hard to judge in the dark, but after a few tries, I felt wind pushing at the back of my head. "Now, Amy!" I shouted. "Lift."

There was a rustling noise as she shoved the front of the shelter up. The wind grabbed us. We jumped forward, and then started racing, bouncing up and down over the waves in the dark. I was glad we didn't have a real sail. This was scary enough. The life raft was a roller coaster with no lights on.

It worked great for a while. But then the wind picked up even more, and we started lifting off the high waves. We'd pound down with a bone-rattling thump, only to have the wind pick us up again. Still, the lightning grew closer.

The rain caught up with us. It spattered my bare

arms and back. I hardly noticed it, since the lightning was so close.

But Cory figured it out. He whispered "Water," in a harsh voice.

Of course! This was rain. Sweet, drinkable rain. I turned my face up and tried to catch as much of it on my tongue as I could. As the rain fell faster, it washed some of the salt crust from my skin.

"Get the container," Cory said. "I'll hold the rudder."

So I fumbled around the edge of the raft until I found where had fastened the container into place. It was still upright, and already filling with rain.

The bottom of the raft was wet now, growing slippery. Bits of seaweed floated around the soles of my feet. We'd need to bail soon. For now, I couldn't face the thought of throwing away fresh water.

I took a long drink from the container, and helped Cory and Amy do the same. Not too much, I told them, or we'd throw up. But we each drank enough to take the tightness from our throats. Then I put the container back into place to collect more water.

The wind blew harder. The water in the raft rose to our ankles. Soon we were fighting for balance. The boat flew off each wave and slammed down onto the next one. "Tanner!" Amy shouted. "No more!"

The lightning seemed to be following a narrow path. If we moved a little to the side, we might escape it. But I didn't know how to do that. Our sail only worked one way.

We needed a new sail.

"I need Dad's windbreaker," I yelled to Amy.

"What?"

"Your jacket! I need it," I shouted. "Cory, help her."

Amy had to remove her life jacket to get the windbreaker off. I held the rudder steady so Cory could help her. He was stronger than I was. But even a day ago, I wouldn't have trusted him to do it.

Cory helped Amy back into her life jacket, then handed me the windbreaker. I shook my head. "You have to be the sail, Cory. You're bigger," I shouted. I told him to zip it up, then pull it over his arms and head, like a t-shirt.

He started to pull it on.

"Not all the way," I said. "Hold it straight up over your head and stretch it as wide as you can." He did, and a gust of wind nearly blew him out of the boat. No standing, then. It wasn't safe. "You have to kneel in the middle, and I'll tell you which way to turn."

"You're crazy!" he shouted.

Maybe. But it was our only chance that I could see. "Amy will hold your legs," I told him. "You have to trust us."

"You're trying to kill me. I'm not doing this!" A flash of lightning, closer now, showed me his face. He was wide-eyed. Scared to death.

I waited for the thunder to pass. It was only one second now, between lightning and thunder. Too close. "It's this, or lie down and wait for the storm," I said.

It was too dark for me to see him. He squeezed my arm. "Aye aye, Skipper," he said.

It was a crazy idea. It was crazy and dangerous and it should never have worked. But it did.

I steered the rudder and shouted directions to Cory. He turned left or right when I told him to, and somehow didn't fall over. Bit by bit, wave by wave, we worked our way out of the path of the storm.

When we reached quieter waves, we used our hands to bail as much water out of the raft as we could.

And then we drifted, waiting to see what morning brought us. Amy was asleep, and I thought Cory was, too, when his voice broke the silence. "We make a good team, Tanner," he said. "You, me, your sister.

Maybe together we'll get out of this alive."

I smiled in the dark. "Yeah, maybe," I replied. The clouds had broken up. We could see the stars now, millions of them. For a long time, we just looked up at them.

If he was wrong, though, if we didn't make it, there was something I wanted Cory to know. "My dad had a ring," I said. "I found it in his stuff. I'm pretty sure he was planning to propose to your mom."

Cory didn't answer right away. "I think . . . that might have been all right," he said. "If they'd gotten married. It might be okay to have a brother and sister."

Cory, Amy and I. We made an okay team. Would we have made an okay family? Maybe. "We'll never know, will we?" My chest tightened.

"Don't give up on your dad," Cory said. He yawned. "Don't give up on us, Tanner. It's a big ocean. But there are a lot of boats out here. By now, a lot of them are looking for us."

"Sure," I said. After a few minutes, Cory's breathing evened out. He was asleep.

I wrapped my arms around my knees.

Cory was right about one thing. It was a big ocean.

Chapter 14

Where the Boats Are

Cory shook me awake the next morning. "It's Amy. It's her leg," he said.

It had been Amy's turn to watch for planes or boats after him. But when Cory shook her to wake her up, she screamed. The two of them had taken off the bandage to see what was wrong.

I couldn't believe I'd slept through all that. But then, I'd stayed on watch until dawn.

Now Amy leaned against the side of the boat in the half that wasn't covered. Her face was red and blotchy. The peeled-back dressing showed that the cut on her leg was even worse than it had been. The cut was red and swollen. Yellow pus oozed around the edges. It was pretty gross. And scary, because of where we were.

"It's hot," Amy said. Her chin shook. "That's bad, isn't it?"

I held my hand just above it and felt the heat coming off. "It's not that bad," I said. "Not yet." But it didn't take a doctor to know that the infection was worse. We had no medicine here. We couldn't even clean it properly.

Cory spat over the edge of the raft. "Where are all the stupid boats and planes? They have to know we're out here. Isn't anybody looking for us?"

Cory was right to be angry. Skipper Jack had made a radio call in the storm. Hadn't anyone heard? He had to file some kind of plan before we left. Somebody would have to know that we didn't make it. There had to be somebody searching for us.

Then I had an idea. "Close to shore," I said.

Cory blinked and looked at me. "They're looking for us close to shore?"

"No. But that's where boats are. The closer we get to shore, the better our chance of being spotted." I dug through our supplies and held up the compass.

"One question, Tanner. Which way is the shore? A compass is only good if you know where you're going."

"We started out between Florida and the Bahamas, right?" I said. "So if we keep going west, we have a good chance of hitting Florida."

"I think we're north of there," Amy said. "I'm pretty sure we're in the Gulf Stream." At our blank looks, she shrugged. "Warm water flowing north-east," she explained. "We covered that in fifth grade."

I rolled my eyes. "So, Florida or Virginia, I don't care. Do you, Cory?" We had sailed our way out of a storm. Why couldn't we sail our way to rescue?

We worked out our direction with the compass. Then we each had a drink of water and took up our sailing positions from last night.

I knew it was a long shot. We were probably wasting our time. But Amy needed help for the cut on her leg. And it felt good to be doing something, instead of just waiting. Cory looked at me and grinned, and I was pretty sure he was thinking the same thing.

We lasted about three hours, with Cory as the sail, Amy anchoring him, and me at the rudder. By then Amy's forehead was hot, Cory was exhausted from standing, and I'd just plain had enough. All that work, and we didn't seem to be getting anywhere. The sun was almost directly overhead and roasting us. There wasn't even much wind.

I made Amy drink some more water and sent her under the shelter to rest.

Cory sat beside me. "It was a good try," he said. He had taken hold of the rudder, and was holding it steady in the water. He glanced at Amy, so fast I almost missed it. Cory was worried about her.

"Suit yourself," I said. But that didn't really cover it. "Cory – thanks."

But he wasn't listening to me. He heard something else. "Airplane!" he shouted.

Chapter 15

Signal Fire

I sat up. "What?"

"Airplane," Cory repeated. "I hear it. Don't you?"

When I listened hard, I could hear it. There was a low-pitched hum. But I couldn't see the plane.

"There." Cory pointed.

It was high overhead. The sun dazzled my eyes when I tried to look at it for too long. What were the chances of them seeing us?

"Get the mirror!" Cory said.

Of course. The signal mirror. I found the mirror and handed it to Cory. He started flashing it around, trying to signal the plane. But what if that wasn't enough? It hadn't worked last time.

We needed something bigger. Something no one could miss. Something like a flare. I looked at our makeshift rudder. What if we set the wood on fire? If it worked, the smoke might be seen. If it didn't work, we'd have lost our rudder.

I shook Amy awake, careful to touch only her good leg. Even her other leg, though, was hot to the touch. "What?" she snapped. Which was weird for Amy. She always woke up happy.

"Can I borrow your glasses?" I asked.

She fumbled around in her pockets and handed them to me. "Careful," she said.

I unfastened the board from the paddle. The wood was still damp from last night. That was good. If I could get it burning, it might smoke more. Maybe we could burn seaweed, too. Leaves made campfires smoky. I wasn't sure if the same was true for seaweed, but it was worth a try.

Cory kept signaling with the mirror. I held Amy's glasses so that the sun shone through the lens and made a tiny, bright spot near one end of the board. After a few moments, it began to smoke. Not enough . . . not nearly enough. I looked up at the plane.

I moved the glasses lens farther away from the

board. Now the bright spot was only a pinprick.

And finally, finally, it caught. A small flame flickered at the end of the board. I shielded it with my hand to let it grow.

Amy passed me a bit of dried seaweed. If it were a campfire, I'd have fed it tiny twigs, but maybe this was the next best thing. I lay the seaweed across the board. The fire flared up around it, but only for a second. It turned the seaweed to a twisted black line.

"Don't," Cory said. "If a spark melts a hole in the raft, we're dead."

My breath caught. What if my plan to get us rescued got us killed? I moved the board slowly, carefully, out past the edge of the raft. Now, if it shot sparks, it could do it in the ocean.

The wood was burning pretty well now. Crackling. A thin stream of gray woodsmoke twisted its way up into the sky. But it wasn't enough. We needed something that would burn messy.

The engine fire, back on the *Sparta*, had burned messy. Lots of smoke, thick and black. That was what we needed. That hadn't come from the wood, though. That had been the oils and plastics and things in the engine. Man-made stuff. Not natural.

We were all barefoot in the boat, but we had our shoes. "Amy," I said. "I need your sandals." They were made of black plastic and webbing.

She passed them to me, and I looped one over the burning end of the stick.

The sandal caught fire. It didn't last long before it dropped into the ocean, but the sandal made thick, oily smoke before it went. Quickly I did the next one. Another thirty seconds of smoke.

Cory and I had damp sneakers. I didn't know if they'd burn or put the fire out. Still, I tried with one of mine. It sent up dark, smudgy smoke, but didn't really burn, except for the shoelaces. The smoke was what we needed.

And all the time, Cory kept signaling with the mirror.

Finally, the plane flew out of sight. I stuck the end of the board in the ocean to put out the flame. We had lost five shoes and burned our board down by about six inches.

We had tried. We had done our best. Now all we could do was sit and wait.

Chapter 16

Still Alive

We gave up on sailing the lifeboat. We wanted to stay close to the spot where we'd sent up the signal. In case it mattered. In case it helped.

So we drifted. Clouds came and went. And, after about an hour, we saw a tiny boat on the horizon. Cory did his trick with the mirror again, and I tried to get another signal fire started.

"It's the last shoe," Cory said as I got it lit.

"Doesn't matter," I told him. "There's nowhere to walk, anyhow."

Cory laughed. We were getting desperate. We'd spent days on the ocean, two of them without food. We'd missed two rescues so far. How many more could we mess up before it was too late?

"Is that mirror doing anything?"

"Yeah," Cory said. He aimed the sun right at my face to make the point. "Sorry," he said, "but you asked."

"Yeah," I said. "But that's it for the smoke. No more shoes. The mirror is all we have left."

I looked over at my sister. "Hey, Amy, we're running out of ideas here. Is there anything . . . Amy? Amy?"

I reached over to give her a shake, but Amy was burning up. Her skin felt like it was on fire. She swatted at me. "Cold," she said. She seemed half asleep.

I grabbed a rag and got it wet in the ocean, then I pressed it to her forehead.

"Amy, come on. Wake up. We're going to make it. . . ."

Then Cory was down next to me. "Keep cooling her down. I'm going to give her some water," he said. "We've got to cut the fever." Cory seemed as worried as I was.

"Yeah, we've got to . . . "

And maybe we did. After five minutes, Amy sat up and looked around. She was still shivering, still too hot, but she was alert.

Only then did we bother to look at the horizon.

Only then did we see that the tiny boat out there had turned.

It was getting bigger. It was coming toward us!

The tiny boat turned out to be a Coast Guard cutter, two storeys high.

Two men on the cutter unhooked a smaller boat from the side and came out to get us. In a few minutes they came up beside our raft.

Cory reached out for the boat as it bumped up against us. "Just a sec," one of the men said. He tied their boat to the raft with ropes. "Don't want to risk anyone going into the drink."

Cory was holding one of Amy's hands; I was holding the other. "Tanner, let go," she said. But I couldn't. What if all this wasn't real?

"Maybe we're seeing things," I said.

Amy shook her head. "They're real," she said.

But I squeezed her hand tighter. Dad had said to protect her. The raft was safe. We had to stay here.

"Tanner." Cory crouched beside me. "Let go of Amy. It's okay."

I looked at him.

"Trust me," he said.

And I did. I let go of Amy's hand. Cory and one

of the coast guard men helped her into the small boat. Then Cory came back for me. We crossed over together.

The small coast guard boat was metal. It was harder than the raft, but it rocked just as much. I sat in the bottom, not trusting my balance on the bench seat. The boat hummed like it was alive.

I heard the two men talking. Something about an airplane, and smoke. They'd seen us, then. Our signal had worked. But the men's voices sounded far away, not quite real. Cory talked to them and I let him.

My lips were dry and cracked. It was hard to get the words out, but there was one thing I needed to ask the men. One question, more important than anything else. "My dad . . ." I began. That was all I could manage.

One of the men grinned. "Your father is on another Coast Guard ship, along with the skipper of that boat you were on. We've been in radio contact. He'll be glad to know we found you. Once we get you onto the main ship, you'll be able to speak with him over the radio. He and the Skipper had quite an adventure. They were found not far from where the ship went down, floating around in their life jackets, strapped together. Good thing the Skipper had a radio beacon."

I smiled. Relief washed over me at last. Dad was okay. We were okay. We had all made it. And we were going home.

It only took us a few hours to reach shore. That didn't seem like much, after all we'd been through. Earlier, I'd been scared to leave the raft. But now I was glad to step on dry land again. I couldn't get down the ramp fast enough.

The wooden dock felt strange under my feet. I had to grab a post for balance. It took me a minute to realize – I wasn't rocking back and forth with the waves anymore.

"Tanner!" It was Dad's voice.

My father looked the same. A little sunburned, but the same. My legs remembered how to run. Soon I was hugging him, and soon after that Amy and Cory were there, too.

All of us. Together.

Epilogue

We became a family six months later, in June. It was a small wedding in a tiny church, but we were all there – even Skipper Jack. Even Mom.

Dad and the Skipper had become good friends. I guess being stranded on the ocean, fighting to stay alive, will do that. It seemed to work for Cory and me.

Skipper Jack offered to let my dad and Cory's mom get hitched on his new sailboat. They said no thanks. None of us wanted to go anywhere near the water for a long time.

Amy was the maid of honor. She got to wear a long dress, which was a good thing because it covered up the scar on her leg. Secretly, though, I think she's proud of the scar. She rolls up her shorts to show it off whenever she gets the chance.

I was my dad's best man with Cory right beside me. He kept tugging at his bow tie as we stood up at the altar. I knew how he felt. My own tie was strangling me.

"Got the rings?" I whispered to him, just as the wedding march began.

He winked. "Don't you trust me?"

I smiled.

Other HIP Xtreme titles to look for

Quake

by ALEX KROPP

When the first earthquake hits, Cyrus is still at home. He leads his sister to safety, then heads to the local hospital to help other victims. That's when the aftershock hits – the second quake that buries him alive.

Lost

by SHARON JENNINGS

Rafe Reynolds thought it would be easy to lead a group of kids into wilderness camping. But soon he's lost in the woods with one of the campers. Together they have to deal with everything from bears and broken bones to anger and fist fights. It all threatens their survival.

Wave

by D.M. OUELLET

Luke and Mai could see the tsunami coming at them, but that didn't give them enough time to get away. When the wave hit, they fought to breathe and fought to reach dry land. And that was only the beginning of the disaster.

Frozen

by LORI JAMISON

Frank and Ray are stranded in the Arctic. Their snowmobile is broken and no one knows where they are. An Arctic storm is coming that can freeze them to death in minutes. The question is simple: how can they survive?

Erin Thomas is the author of two books in the HIP Fantasy collection (*Draco's Fire, Wolves at the Gate*) and other books for reluctant readers. She has never been stranded in a life raft, but did attend sailing camp as a child. Her favorite part of that camp was when the kids were allowed to capsize their boats. Erin lives in Whitby, Ontario, with her husband and daughter. For more information, visit *www.erinthomas.ca*.

For more information on HIP novels:

High Interest Publishing
www.hip-books.com